Mr. Sneakers

by Bob McGrath

Illustrated by Meredith Johnson

PRICE STERN SLOAN
Los Angeles

For his continued good advice, and for taking the time to read and evaluate each story in the Bob's Books series, I would like to thank Dr. Gerald S. Lesser, Professor of Education and Developmental Psychology, Harvard University; Chairman, Board of Advisors, The Children's Television Workshop.

For their sensitive and encouraging input, I would also like to thank the following:

Julia Cummins, Coordinator of Children's Services of the New York Public Library

Dr. Richard Graham, Former Director of the Center for Moral Education and Development at Harvard University

Tom Greening, Ph.D., Editor of the Journal of Humanistic Psychology

Betty Long, Senior Children's Librarian, General Library of the Performing Arts at Lincoln Center (New York Public Library)

Valeria Lovelace, Director of Research - "Sesame Street"

Ann Sperry McGrath, children's book author and preschool teacher

Hannah Nuba, Director of the New York Public Library Early Childhood Resource and Information Center

Lisa Ann Marsoli, Editorial Director — Juvenile Division, Price Stern Sloan

ISBN: 0-8431-2397-4

Library Of Congress Catalog Card Number: 89-30677

10 9 8 7 6 5 4 3 2 1

It was the first day of school, but Teddy felt at home right away because he had gone there for kindergarten and first grade. The day was going pretty smoothly, until a boy in Teddy's class asked him why he was wearing such beat-up sneakers. Teddy looked down at his feet, shrugged his shoulders and said, "Oh, I don't know. I like them this way."

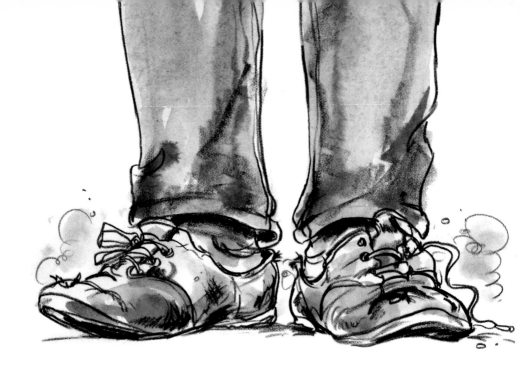

In fact, Teddy had worn those sneakers all summer long and loved them. They were the most comfortable pair of sneakers he had ever put on his feet. And, except to go to bed at night, Teddy hardly ever took them off. He was surprised that anyone had even noticed them, and since nobody else mentioned his sneakers the rest of that day, he forgot about it.

When he went home his mom asked him, "How was your first day at school?"

He said, "Great, Mom."

On the second day of school, all the kids were out in the yard playing kickball when one of the girls on the other team began teasing Teddy. "Hey, Mr. Sneakers," she hollered, "how fast can you run in those things?" She had on brand-new pink high tops.

Teddy thought about the boy who had questioned him the day before, and this time he said, "Plenty fast. They won the twenty-yard dash in the park on Labor Day."

Some of the kids laughed. Teddy wasn't really sure why they were laughing, and he felt a little funny. After school, as he started up the walk to his apartment building, someone said, "Good-bye, Old Sneakers, see you tomorrow."

As he was getting ready to go to bed that night, Teddy's mom asked him how his second day at school went.

He said, "Uh, OK."

She said, "Just OK?" She could tell by the tone of his voice that something was bothering him.

He said, "Almost everything was OK. It's just that some of the kids—," and then he stopped. "Mom, do you like my sneakers?"

His mom said, "Sure, Teddy, but what has that got to do with anything?"

He said, "Well, I think that some of the kids were teasing me about them."

"How?" his mom asked.

"Well," he said, "I noticed that some of the kids were laughing and pointing at my sneakers when I walked past them and a couple of them called me 'Mr. Sneakers' in the playground."

His mom just listened quietly while Teddy explained. Then she asked him, "What are the other kids wearing?"

"I guess they all got new sneakers for the first day of school," he answered.

"How's your big toe?" she asked.

"My big toe loves these sneakers as much as I do," he said.

She laughed and said, "No, I meant do your sneakers still fit you, or does your big toe hit the end?"

"Mom, they fit fine. They're the best sneakers I've ever had in my whole life," he said.

"They are getting a little bit ragged," she suggested.

"Yeah, but who cares?" he said. "They feel great and I can do anything in them. They really grip the sidewalk and they go as fast as a skateboard."

"Yes, but you know, Teddy, sometimes kids are very fussy about sneakers. They like to have just the right color, and the right laces. I guess they all want to look the same," she said.

"I know, but I like these sneakers, Mom," he said.

"There's nothing wrong with wearing old sneakers," she said. "So if you like them and you want to wear them, then wear them."

On the third day of school, nobody mentioned Teddy's sneakers until they were lined up to leave the lunch room. Then somebody looked down at all the sneakers and began to sing, "One of these things is not like the others . . . "

Teddy looked around and realized that everybody was staring at his feet. Then they all began giggling as though it was the funniest joke
they had ever heard. Teddy didn't feel like
laughing at all. He wanted to shrug his shoulders and pretend that he thought it was funny
too, but he couldn't.

Instead he said, "These are my best, favorite
sneakers. They're winning sneakers. I wore
them to camp. I wore them in a canoe. I wore
them when I caught a really big fish, and I
wore them when I climbed a mountain. I've had
fun in these sneakers. And besides, my mom
says, if I like them, I can wear them."

On the way home from school, Lily, a girl from Teddy's class, started walking with him. "Teddy, did you really do all that stuff this summer that you told us about, like fishing and mountain climbing?" she asked.

And Teddy said, "Yup."

At dinner his mother asked, "How'd your old sneakers like school today?"

Teddy said, "Fine, I told everyone about what my sneakers did this summer at day camp."

"Did you tell them they got stuck in the mud and turned black?" she asked.

"No, I think I forgot that part," he grinned.

"I thought you might," she smiled back. "That's 'cause you didn't have to clean them."

"Thanks again, Mom," Teddy said, and gave her a big kiss.

On Thursday and Friday, Teddy waited to see what would happen. It didn't take long. Both days, even in the playground before the bell rang, three girls walked by and said, "Hi, Mr. Sneakers."

Teddy just smiled at them and said, "Do you want to race?"

At spelling time, the teacher asked them to spell rhyming words. The kids began to giggle again and spelled "sneaker," "creaker" and "squeaker."

Teddy wondered for a moment if wearing his old sneakers was really worth all the kidding.

He thought about it again and he decided he really liked them. He stood up, looked at his classmates, and slowly spelled out, "fleeter: F.L.E.E.T.E.R. That means faster.

Teddy's teacher laughed and said, "That's called a 'forced rhyme', but it sounds enough alike to be able to use it."

At lunch some of the kids began to tap their feet on the floor under the table. It sounded like thirty basketball players running down the court. Teddy knew they were teasing him again and wondered what he was going to do about it this time, when Mrs. Pinsak, who was in charge of the lunch room, said, "Enough of that noise!" And they had to stop. Teddy was glad about that.

At gym class Teddy won the long jump, the speed race and the one-legged hop. In fact, he won almost all the events that the teacher gave them that day.

On the way home from school on Friday, Lily, the same little girl who had asked him if he had really done all those things at camp, said to him, "What else did you do in those sneakers?"

Teddy said, "Well, I climbed trees. I rode my bike and I got stuck in the mud."

That night at dinner his mother said, "Well, how did Mr. Sneakers do today?"

Teddy said, "Oh, Mom, not you, too! I heard too much about my sneakers all week."

Then his mother said, "I'm sorry, Teddy. Does it bother you that much? We can get you some new sneakers tomorrow."

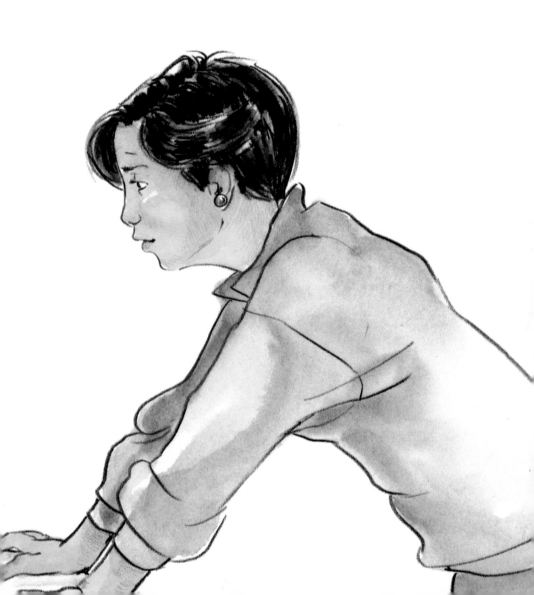

"Yeah, it's beginning to bother me, but I'm never going to take off my best sneakers," he said in a determined voice. "They make my feet feel good."

"Sometimes it's pretty tough not to do the same thing that everybody else is doing," his mom said, "especially when kids tease you and try to make you do it. It looks to me as if you have made up your mind and you're doing what you think is right."

They sat there quietly for a moment and then Teddy smiled and said, "You're right, Mom, that's just what I'm doing."

Teddy sounded determined when he was talking to his mother, but as he was getting
dressed for school on Monday morning, he
stopped and looked at his sneakers and
thought, What's going to happen today? I won-
der what the kids are going to call me? If I got
new ones, no one could call me "Mr. Sneakers."

But, he thought about the talk with his mom, and he picked up his old sneakers, pulled the tongues up good and tight, and tied the laces up to the top. They felt just right.

However, when he reached the sidewalk and saw some of the kids, he decided not to catch up with them. When he arrived at school, he waited by the schoolyard gate until the bell rang so that he would be the last in line.

That morning the teacher called each of them up, one by one, to tell what they had done on the weekend. The first person to go to the front of the class was Lily. She began to talk about the picnic she had gone to that weekend with her cousins.

She was in the middle of telling how they had cooked marshmallows on long sticks over a fire, when Teddy noticed that everyone was staring at her feet and whispering. He leaned into the aisle so he could see her better, and was amazed when he saw that she had on the oldest pair of sneakers that he had ever seen. They were even more worn out and scruffier than his.

Lily kept on talking. "As you can see, I am wearing my summer sneakers. These are the sneakers that I wore to the picnic. I had such a good time in them that I decided to wear them to school today. I also decided that it's OK to wear them to school whenever I want to, just like Teddy does."

The room was very quiet. Teddy couldn't believe what he was hearing. What's going to happen now, he thought. He could hardly wait until they went outside. No one said anything to him.

As soon as Lily was alone he walked over to her and said, "I'm glad you wore your old sneakers today."

Lily smiled and said, "These are my championship jump-roping sneakers. I couldn't jump rope with my new sneakers, not until they're broken in. I feel good in these sneakers. And I'm glad you've been wearing yours. It made me feel OK about wearing mine."

"Guess what?" Teddy said.

"What?" Lily answered.

"I don't know how to jump rope."

"You don't?" Lily looked surprised.

"Nope," Teddy said.

"But you can climb trees and mountains," Lily said. "And you can ride bikes and win races and get stuck in the mud. So you won't have any trouble jumping rope. Sneakers like ours are just perfect for jumping rope."

Just then the gym teacher blew her whistle and they both began to run.